THE HOUSE
AT THE END OF THE ROAD

For my parents, and in memory of my grandparents — K.R.

Owlkids Books acknowledges the financial support of the Canada Council for the Arts, the Ontario Arts Council, the Government of Canada through the Canada Book Fund (CBF) and the Government of Ontario through the Ontario Creates Book Initiative for our publishing activities.

Published in Canada by
Owlkids Books Inc.
1 Eglinton Avenue East
Toronto, ON M4P 3A1

Published in the United States by
Owlkids Books Inc.
1700 Fourth Street
Berkeley, CA 94710

Library and Archives Canada Cataloguing in Publication

Rust, Kari, author, illustrator
        The house at the end of the road / Kari Rust.
ISBN 978-1-77147-335-4 (hardcover)
        I. Title.
PS8635.U883H68 2019   jC813'.6   C2018-906591-5

Library of Congress Control Number: 2018963953

Editor Karen Li
Designer Danielle Arbour

ONTARIO ARTS COUNCIL
CONSEIL DES ARTS DE L'ONTARIO
an Ontario government agency
un organisme du gouvernement de l'Ontario

Canada Council   Conseil des Arts
for the Arts   du Canada

Canada

Manufactured in Shenzhen, Guangdong, China, in March 2019, by WKT Co. Ltd.
Job #18CB2646

A   B   C   D   E   F

Owl kids   Publisher of Chirp, Chickadee and OWL | Owlkids Books is a division of   bayard canada
          www.owlkidsbooks.com

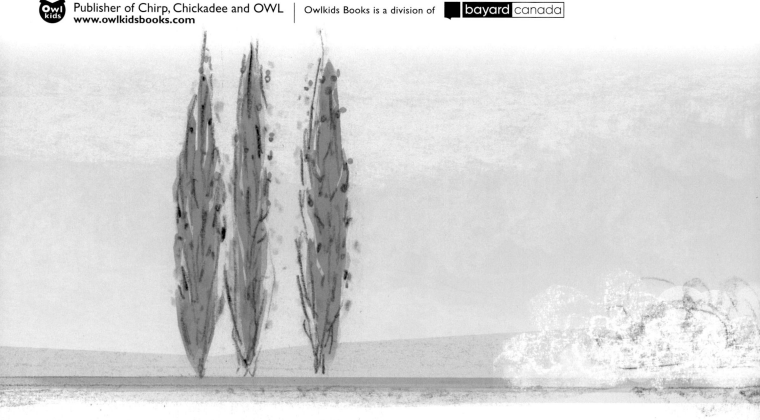

The House
at the End of the Road

Kari Rust

Owlkids Books

Robert, do I hear
bouncing again?

Every summer, my brother, Patrick,
and I visit our grandma.
Our cousin Robert is usually there
at the same time. He stays
with Grandma a lot.

I don't think Robert really wanted to break the glass. The rock just tapped the window and skipped into the gutter. Suddenly...

A ghost!

And then
we had a
problem.

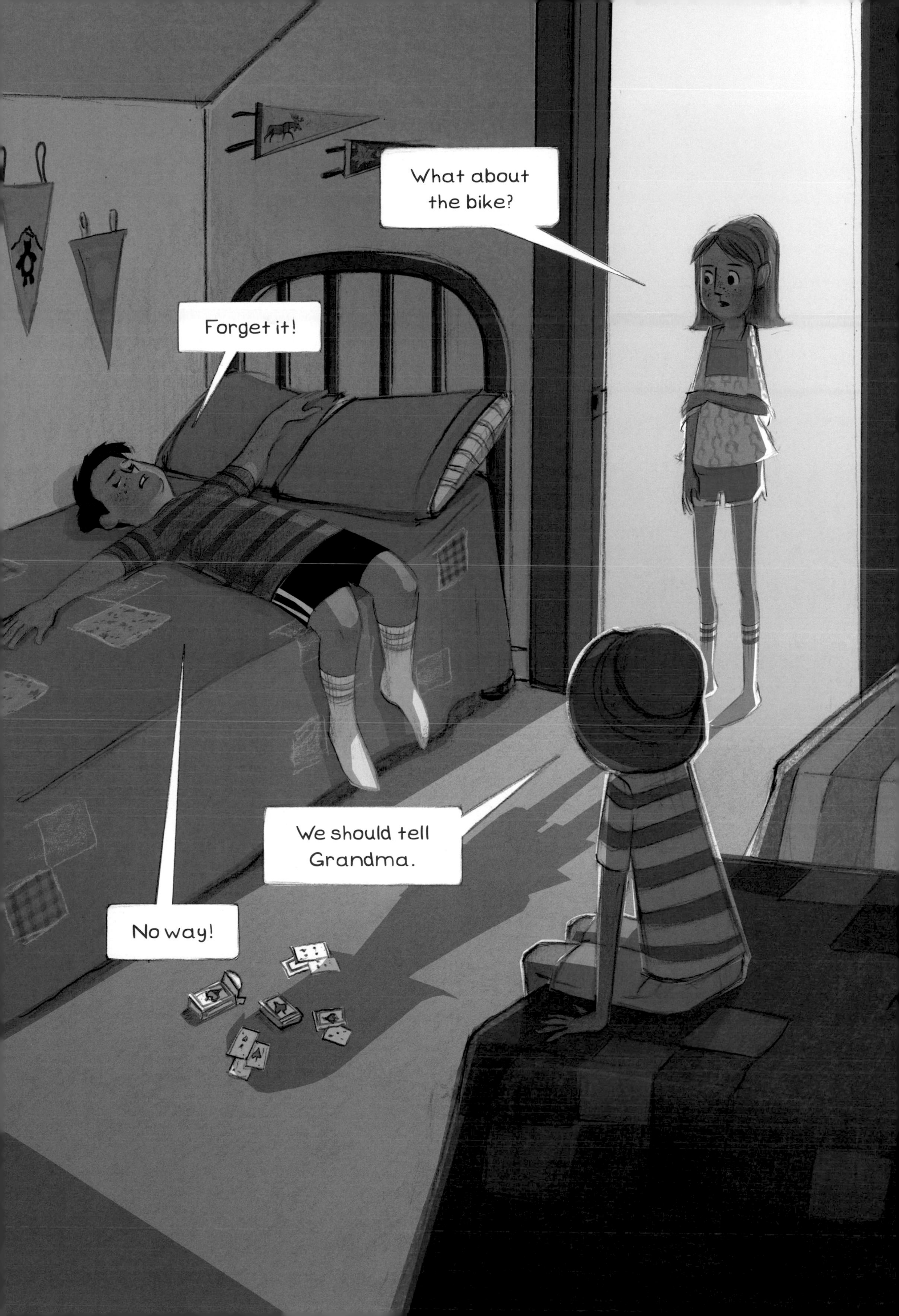
What about the bike?
Forget it!
We should tell Grandma.
No way!

The next day, we *had* to tell Grandma.

Grandma said it was the Old Peterson House.
Mr. Peterson had been Grandma's favorite teacher
when she was a girl. But he wasn't a ghost.

I'll take you there after
breakfast. You three can apologize,
and we'll pick up the bike.

Where is that child?

We were all pretty nervous.

I hope Grandma's sure about that ghost.

Come along, now.

He invited us inside the old house.

It was full of fascinating things. Each one had a story.

There were films that played
on a whirring projector
and piles of old books about
plants and animals.

Some had flowers pressed
in them from years before.

Mr. Peterson showed us toys that moved without batteries and an old photograph of a swimming hole.

We could hardly believe *he* was the boy in the striped bathing suit!

When it was time to go, Mr. P. gave us each a gift.

An old camera for Robert.
Beautiful pencils and a notebook for me.
Gardening tools for Patrick.
And an old-fashioned board game for Grandma.

We visited the old house
a lot over the summer.
We loved its cool, dark
basement,

its creaky attic,

... And its tumbledown garden,
still pretty in its own way.

Then one day, Mr. Peterson
wasn't there.

Instead, there was a man posting a sign on the door. He said that the house was old and unsafe. Mr. Peterson had been moved out.

No!

Grandma found out that Mr. Peterson was taken
to a retirement house by the river. He'd caught
a bad cold, so no visitors for two weeks.

By then, summer would be over and we'd be gone.

We decided to go back and save Mr. P.'s things.
But we were too late. Everything was gone.

Robert stormed off.

Patrick found a little tin under
the porch and started filling it
with seeds and clippings from
the old garden.

Maybe we *could* save
something for Mr. P.
I sat down and started to write.

That evening, Robert came back
so late he almost missed dinner.

He finally showed up with an envelope of photos
he had taken. The pictures were of ordinary things
around Mr. P.'s house, but somehow Robert had
made them look beautiful.

Robert was full of surprises!

We packed our collections
in a box before we left.

Grandma promised to deliver our package to Mr. Peterson.

And she did.

I can hardly wait
for next summer.